Down East IN THE Ocean

A Maine Counting Book

WRITTEN BY **PETER** AND **CONNIE ROOP**
ILLUSTRATED BY **NICOLE FAZIO**

Down East

ISBN 978-0-89272-709-4

Library of Congress Cataloging-in-Publication Information available on request

Design by Chad Hughes

Printed in Singapore

5 4 3 2 1

Down East

Distributed to the trade by National Book Network

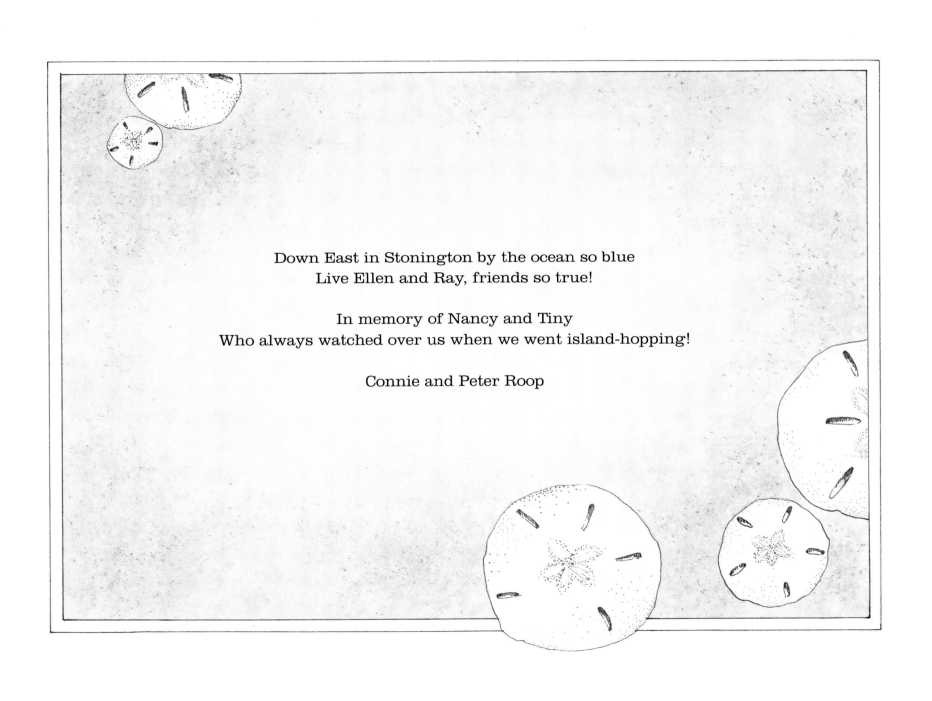

Down East in Stonington by the ocean so blue
Live Ellen and Ray, friends so true!

In memory of Nancy and Tiny
Who always watched over us when we went island-hopping!

Connie and Peter Roop

Down East in the ocean,
under Maine's summer sun,
lived a mother seal
and her little seal one.

"Swim," said the mother.
"I swim!" said the one.
So they swam all day under
Maine's summer sun.

1

Down East in the ocean,
in Maine's sea so blue,
lived a mother whale
and her little whales two.

"Spout," said the mother.
"We spout!" said the two.
So they spouted all day
in Maine's sea so blue.

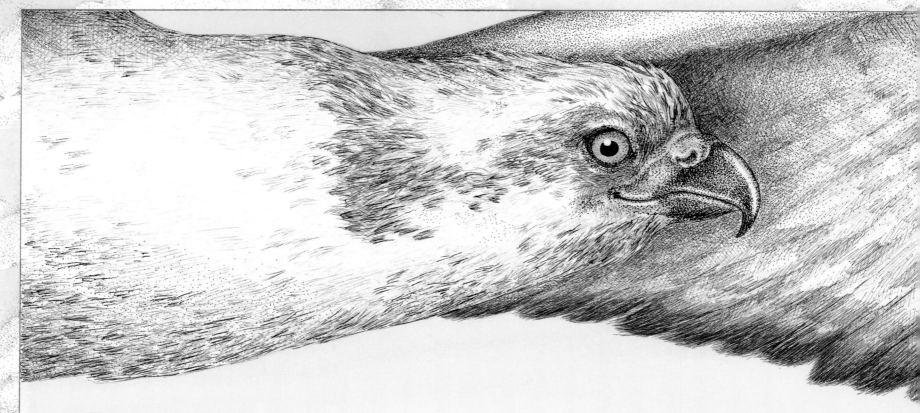

Down East by the ocean,
over a Maine island tree,
lived a mother osprey
and her little ospreys three.

"Fly," said the mother.
"We fly!" said the three.
So they flew all day over
a Maine island tree.

Down East in the ocean,
along Maine's foggy shore,
lived a mother crab
and her little crabs four.

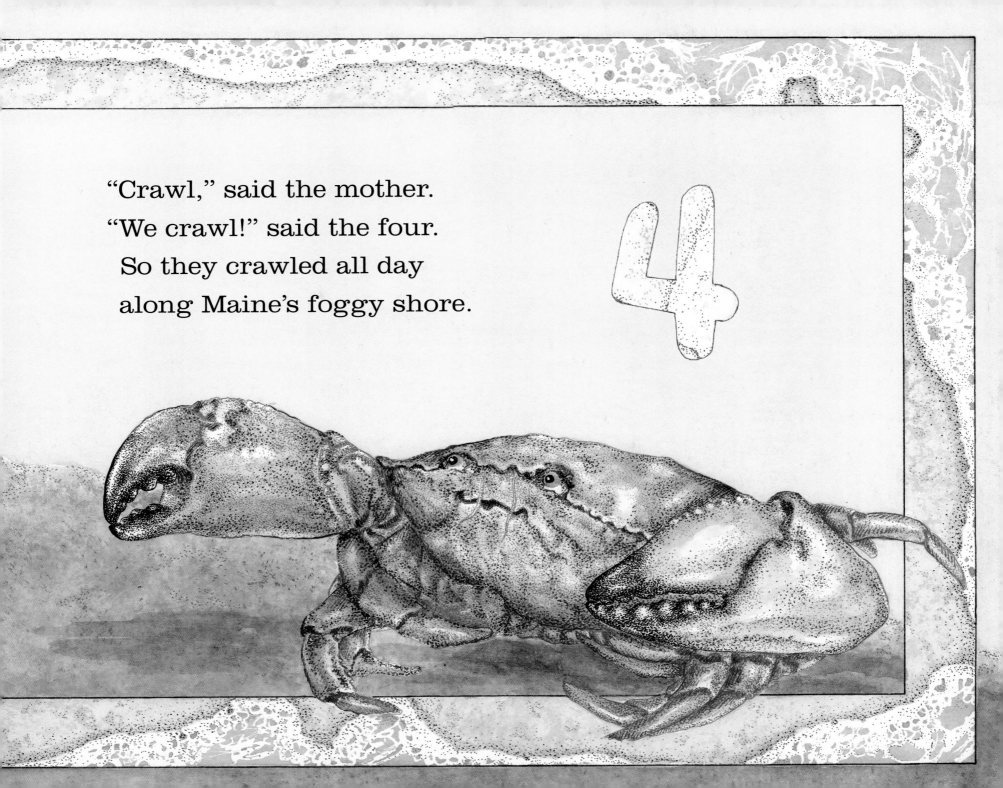

"Crawl," said the mother.
"We crawl!" said the four.
So they crawled all day
along Maine's foggy shore.

Down East in the ocean,
where Maine dolphins dive,
lived a mother jellyfish
and her little jellies five.

"Float," said the mother.
"We float!" said the five.
So they floated all day
where Maine dolphins dive.

Down East by the ocean,
in a Maine nest of sticks,
lived a mother eagle
and her little eagles six.

"Eat," said the mother.
"We eat!" said the six.
So they ate all day in a
Maine nest of sticks.

Down East in the ocean,
under Maine stars of heaven,
lived a mother starfish
and her little stars seven.

"Cling," said the mother.
"We cling!" said the seven.
So they clung all night under
Maine stars of heaven.

Down East in the ocean, in
Maine, the Pine Tree State,
lived a mother clam
and her little clams eight.

"Squirt," said the mother.
"We squirt!" said the eight.
So they squirted all day
in the Pine Tree State.

Down East in the ocean,
in the Maine sunshine,
lived a mother seagull
and her little seagulls nine.

"Laugh," said the mother.
"We laugh!" said the nine.
So they laughed all day
in the Maine sunshine.

Down East in the ocean,
under Maine lobstermen,
lived a mother lobster
and her little lobsters ten.

"Hide," said the mother.
"We hide!" said the ten.
So they hid all day from
the Maine lobstermen.

Down East in the oc - ean, un - der Maine's sum - mer sun, lived a

mo - th - er seal and her lit - tle seal pup one.

"Swim," said the moth - er. "I swim!" said the one. So they

swam all day un - der Maine's sum - mer sun.